Francis Mutemwa wrote *Sigh* while taking courses for digital and media production. Born in Kenya, he moved to the United States when he was 13. Since he was young, he developed a great attention for the arts. As a trilingual, Francis ought to connect the dots incorporated with social growth through the extensive studies of literature and economic branches. While working on his dissertation to prove that randomization had a decimal pattern, he recognized the conversion of abstract art in its own provisions. As an attempt to ease the adverse potentiality of symbolism, Francis hoped to publish his theory to art students and later the world.

I was especially inspired by the Federation of Asia-Pacific Air Cargo Association and the optimism that may be pushing them every day.

Francis Mutemwa

SIGH

AUSTIN MACAULEY PUBLISHERS™

LONDON • CAMBRIDGE • NEW YORK • SHARJAH

Ordering Information
Quantity sales: Special discounts are available on quantity purchases by corporations, associations, and others. For details, contact the publisher at the address below.

Publisher' Cataloging-in-Publication data
Mutemwa, Francis
Sigh

ISBN 9781638297727 (Paperback)
ISBN 9781638297734 (ePub e-book)

Library of Congress Control Number: 2023903123

www.austinmacauley.com/us

First Published 2023
Austin Macauley Publishers LLC
40 Wall Street, 33rd Floor, Suite 3302
New York, NY 10005
USA

mail-usa@austinmacauley.com
+1 (646) 5125767

Table of Contents

Chapter 1

0 to 29 Miles

In the open seas are three mega cargo ships named Vessel by brush, Opliet, and Mike does. Within rocky waters, variations of turbulence and dangerous mechanical attributes lay to be tampered with.

A system of map navigation is set in place for visual confirmation and gadgets adjusted to the telemetry of nautical capabilities.

While ripping through, tropically sent winds navigators have to keep up with communications at intervals as to keep their waypoint planner updated.

Chapter 2

29 to 58 Miles

Carrying eight, the *vessel by brush* waited alongside the port. An Irishman named Huey stands slender and lacks a frail look who is the master. Ileck, pronounced aiy-lek, is the first mate with black hair containing ringlets with an average height, and has strong hands. Vata, pronounced as var-tar, who happens to be the bosun has jet black wispy hair short and square hands. Nermis, pronounced naa-miss; the chief engineer, has a herculean body type carrying plump hands fashioning a butterscotch untamed hair and cornering his cheeks with a goatee. The second engineer's name is Buid, pronounced boo-ee-d, has an overbite that is clean-shaven, carries long midnight hair and is built with a barrel-chest.

Utvu, pronounced oot-voo; is the medical purser, is chubby and has white bushy hair, narrow lips under a crooked nose with a catlike face. Mect, pronounced mek-t, is an elongated face equipped with lush lips adjacent to a beard and is the cook. Nioler, pronounced nee-oh-lar, has a soft face hanging with raw skin, snub nose, keeps moist lips with an afro that's inky black and is the watch leader.

This team puts a nonchalant aura around the ship on and off watch. With the exuberance of the cook and the bosun, life comes out to be livable at lengthy cross-oceanic trips.

Chapter 3

58 to 87 Miles

Doe, pronounced do-u-w; the master of Opliet, has freckles, ash brown tangled hair, and is tall with rugged nails. Fotrs, pronounced four-tris; Opliet's first mate, has elegant hands, fit body, sandy blond hair, and straight teeth hooked to a strong face. Herma is the bosun, pronounced har-ma; has raw skin and arched brows with a silent personality, sharp eyes. Tastie, one of the cooks, pronounced tasty, is slim and has a rash understanding on the manufacturing of ship engines and has expertise on medicine making her a medical purser. Eeku, the second engineer, pronounced yee-koo is chubby with blonde hair. Gollow, pronounced go-low, is the other cook and has blonde hair and delicate eyes. Rimblae, the watch leader, has a substance of new words with a knack of spelling them. Rumson has a cliff-hanging attribute with how she put things. Gos, pronounced goss, is a geology specialist and moves around with a broken accent. This makes up Opliet's full crew.

Chapter 4

87 to 110 Miles

Ovas cornered and straight with steel. A trace of mitigation. Partially convenient. Modest of the cane.

Eruq, an opposing fanatic, knew Pewter as a counselor of a rendition. Finding a rested assured point of a posture. A turn of a controlled course. A bubbling steam stabilization of a concern.

Balchae, pronounced ball-kay, fuming at the cause of probability. Situations arranged for a moment. Regards for the tone as a devious act. Pointed as the connections of a labyrinth's upbringing set of cliffs. Pulling toward a resemblance of composition declared by its image of crushed sides.

Getlet opinion rolled into turmoil. As a candidate, the making of a treacherous mood sent toward a compelling static abundance at the feet of an isle contesting. Past complications rocked the grapple defining a sequence. Devices concerning a brightly luminous sound. A valid covalence at the matching of compression. An oddly returning confession. A lid marking a figment mentioning what is given.

Duis pronounced doo-ees, with cocoa brown eye dark brows that spoke loudly.

Repe carried a shadow of insufficiency.

Bedar broke a rowdy plummeting arrow sharp for its own fall.

Fau has a needle for the thing it took to spot a raise.

Mike does wrote an echo about a retaliative surrounding.

The Master decayed on an onslaught of proportions, First Mate; the consciousness hook of the weight. Bosun left a ring in the heads. The Chief Engineer, Second Engineer, and the Medical Purser were taken by the ratings of personalities. Cook and Watch Leader are being left eye to eye.

Chapter 5

110 to 145 Miles

Toiling efforts grow as luggages are strapped to the ground inside *Vessel by brush*. Calculated frontal positioning at the mask of its crew strung the date.

A long list of premonitions flew inside Gollow's head since the departure rush had coincided with every other plan she could have made.

"Call in departure and set in a 30-minute warning." A voice was heard while the bask of an interior promoted its own secrecy.

Timid escalation of excitement with every crewmember rose every second.

A risk at the commentary of awe floated in the founding of a new journey.

"That's when I forgot to take a ride out into the country," Huey, the captain, told Illeck.

Coded readmission at the platforms of friendship gazed at *Vessel by brush's* crew.

"I couldn't afford it," Vata summarized her last night. An affordable element representing the lay of isolation between seduction and psychological gluttony.

A pronunciation above intrinsic sound waves grouped the crew members.

Conferences in an issued point were inbound. Counting the conventional rate of waves was on the schedule for the first mate bottom eyelid. Counted by an installment is the propellers bubbles while docked. Plummeting at the contest of calamity is the height of zero elevation from the deck. An allegation of a track was painted where crew members walk inside the ship. Centered by the caves that altered sensation is the hope for safety during their voyage.

Chances at retribution were expected at the sincerity of goodbyes. Compared to a dull auction of an appearance is the pale grey color of the wide sides of *Vessel by brush*. Curves between efforts sharpened the look of a black tinted three-hundred-and-forty-five-meter ship. An acute statement holding its own name 'Vessel by brush,' posing as a commenting location rover. A connection of bribery was held between the one that was leasing this ship and its owner.

Marking up an edition was a hue of a journey.

Content with a willow's leaf bended before someone could broom it off.

A transpired reminder rang; one similar to other horns.

Bringing up the aisle that stood for a competitive attendance.

"You're in the center," the captain's voice was heard over the speakers directing the last crate alignment on a crane.

A moment rested to equip a format of branding and shining facts resting in the checklist.

Utvn found efforts being exaggerated since it was only the first day. Memorized by a state of body language he could tell tactics that conserve energy. Finalized by the stature one could still be applicable for more than a bed rest succeeding the ports and stern assignments.

Publicized reimagination grew for the creativity used to endure sailing the western Pacific. Pure formats of reinstallation were needed between crew member's jokes and small talks for psychological stabilization between each other. Accusing the center of the membrane rested a shrug of boredom. An agenda of promotion still haunted the captain from the crew's succeeding trips. Concerned by an astute form of sea sickness; some chose to chew herbs. Cordless accessorizing ought to be a mix up since wireless frequencies could be intercepted.

A lasting farewell at the goodbye of the freight ship.

An order at the boarding allegiance; welcoming a greater tone of footsteps from a quiet timeout while docked.

Drenching an upward form of vision *vessel by brush* stood. Dual evidence between witnesses was unknowingly exchanged. Coincidence around the pull of a falling apart departure.

Chapter 6

145 to 174 Miles

Cornering limits grew with Opliet. Regenerating decimals invested in the authentication of the three-hundred-and-five-meter ship.

Simplicity relinquished equipped an attempt to breed anonymity while withstanding the girth of its size.

Bold effort for the conservation of a leap over a heat within urgency defined the hum of the turbines at rest priorly to leaving the port with a six-foot piece of jewelry. Poise at a resemblance as it was one out of three. Minimal decadence talked of for the security of its harboring. While on land, it was bestowed at an exterior calling module.

Positive conditioning from Doe and the rest of the crew as an elaborate confession for the level of security needed. Costly weight being dragged across the pacific for a cosmetic insertion for the Eik Isle resort in Alaska.

Just mannerism left it standing stout. Lacking a forward angle; a hard and rigid piece of sculpture. This piece of diamond stored an age of the commission. A plaque of an astute profession within many. Desolate mitigation bribed for the loose send off.

Leaving a fork shaped mist as it's lifted its connections to others was almost a fever. Its price is a content that stands upright and sadistic compared to others. It is a delightful connection of relationships.

Its pigment hosts members of a modified structure. A walk away hosts minutes founded by a grant force. Other gems are crowded by a similar compression formula. It usually is suspected to be forming the glues flight path under less dense air vapors. It's usually borrowing a slate pasted by the content while resting on its base.

Chapter 7

174 to 203 Miles

Pinnacles at the grounds marked the forthcoming trip. At a rounded spark, the ship's name *Mike does,* glows. Recently completing a dusty makeup from a full maintenance check managed by its captain.

The captain, Ovas, stood concerned about the junk pile declining by numbers relieving himself from the ignorance of not knowing what the ship had collected.

Hearing a thrust marked *Mike does's* departure across the pacific. Pounds of limiting weight defined the three-hundred-and-fifteen-foot ship.

Viscosity on the promotional possibilities laying on the crew members' shoulders. Tranquil and opposed, the crew and the ship walked the traffic waters. Marine courage reflected by their banners hanging off flagpoles. Wine toasts and cadence playing off the speakers accompanied the dialogue shared as *Mike does* sailed out. Navigational limits indulging as a relinquished format of inserting the location of the ship being used as top priority.

Pouches under every seat stood as security for the placements of handheld objects at the mobility of crew members.

Jaws carrying an echo underwater from the ship.

Parts of an instructional packet mentioned sleeping hours and incentives of the voyage. While bending what had a personal relationship for every member, the night fell fast.

A riddle inside of an ominous carriage floated around as a symbol of the trait of communication between crew members during their voyage.

Chapter 8

203 to 232 Miles

Rounded at the gratuitous moments marked a circulatory system manned by captains. Finally embedding its crew is the best feeling and most laborious. Impending anguish on a cliff of mentality. Needs of comfort roam about the angles of feng shui for an eighteen-day trip. Opportunities of a posture for a mean regard are needed.

Finesse on an upbringing resting on tackles of stress.

Rolling like a rascal are the senses of humor aboard.

Immediate results aren't needed since the lack of social memes are about to be miles away.

Controversy could be used as a multifunctional resource for evaluation.

Additional counter reactions are a suggestive trait from captains and leads toward crew members. Probable inanimate provisions mark the scenery outside each ship.

Bleek states of hygiene define what is needed for voyages.

Affordable motions of conquest lay to be witnessed.

Chapter 9

232 to 261 Miles

Backing in an insertion inside the waters was the mission statement of *Mike does, Opliet, and vessel by brush* bringing in efforts of continuance. Sadistic approach as the girth and size of the ship over strengthens others. Mentioned as a statute were their logistics logged every five nautical mile. Cross examining the favorable result of the navigation heading was the first mate's duty.

They are minutes used for collateral sailing paths. Frowns weep at the efforts it takes to navigate mega ships. But as experience grows amazement is found in a fluctuation pocket. Guesses of equipment become a jovial form of comparison within the crew members.

Built by sturdy metal the walls remain fortified. Patterns of concern roam only for the lack of fuel due to over correction. A condition of premise lays in between thrill and responsibility on the stern. An amount of insoluble practice; one would define these ships sitting singularly. Opposition dealt with a specified motion directs the bow within rough waves.

Chapter 10

261 to 290 Miles

Equivalence on a stepping-stone appropriated the dash of the ships. The dull effort around the crude forces was weight being dragged above the water. Fine efforts of balance stayed reenacted. Greater than the prime vector of sound the horn was used.

Beneath an effort a subtle ocean sat.

Aiming at the sky the uniforms of crew members struck against all layers of light.

Parameters including a static situation used for communication frequencies. Isolation on each communication device.

Around a stake crowned by rocks by the shore the ships must go. Dusting a corner without overturning.

As a solemn allegiance of a contraption, the crew must remain clung to society's radius of sanity. Vindicated partitions on the convent of nautical topics. An edition of the proclivity rests on responsible shoulders.

Chapter 11

290 to 319 Miles

A sturdy alignment swarming the direction of zero elevation. Bashing at the presence of sound criticism, wheeshing at similar clicks as that of the breath of a dozen sprinting horses, wet and filled with pockets of engaging silence.

The rocks knelt with a confident aggression at the sinking traffic that had a possibility to surrender its surroundings with a deep hum.

Chapter 12

319 to 348 Miles

The concern of voluptuous bubbles by the rudder of Opliet. Conniving escapes indulged inside caves. Caves under water covered by renaissance from the sonar.

A purpose victorious at the epitome of every tenth of a mile completed. Collected form of an isotope was the sense of humor needing to swarm the deck area.

A landscape was still vivid at the isolated participation of awareness of Opliet's crew.

Chapter 13

348 to 377 Miles

Already blended into conniving moments was vessel by brush thirty-hour mark. Prosperity into the decor stood invisible in between the beginning of stressful turns. Support into the corners marched by grain was a state directed toward each crew member about each other.

Mediocre grooves stretched out of ocean life on the iron sides. Collection of vivid stars directing the heading.

"We lit grooms out of pardoning stems." Nermis grew as a correspondent.

"Portions of delicacy." Buid redeemed a source of circumstance.

"Yeah, parts of the crude elements are the reality of things." Nermis stood victorious on the rumble's delightful quest.

"Camping on the docking of a settling tone." Buid laid a statute of chance grew decisively.

The back and forth form of conversation posted a note that states needs and turns of the navigation of an angle. Plaques of an edition.

Redemption as a wit was the aura roaming in and out rooms and the cargo area. Surveillance on a structure sent back to the managerial point. A mockery of a gender-based sense on the floor. Transgressing odor as a welcoming pull. As the past redeems itself on Vessel by brush's ocean path.

Mastered to be a window by a shed the temperatures were fused on the gauges. Constant balancing was grown from side to side. Weight of a tremor could only be heard from a distance. Induced by the common count of freight ships. An agenda of corners was irresistible.

A composition of visual compounding.

Minding the lapse that was seen carrying a hefty weight name was seen as an astute fortress. Left bending sense of oceanic currents spewed as a carpet toward the nine o'clock view of the ship.

Conquest ahead of time was the sense of pride. A chance of a cushion between the more close-knit colleagues.

A draft printed for its regard in the office. Gushing with water condensing composition the engines hummed. Pumping at a higher interval every five miles. Participation of gossip inside of a group. This was a host declared for comparison of a valid term. Contribution as an elaborate scent of ascending water levels.

Buoye existing after each strike of a wave.

Favorite pinpointed location, Kigigaq Island, which was the final destination.

Delicate measure of anguish hadn't risen to evaluation yet; it was six in the morning the next day.

Entangled charisma at the quench of emotion roamed around Mect, the cook.

Attribute of a finish marked the ideal format of the tone of conversations in the cafeteria within the crew.

Parameters at the role of a cost had evaporated and were only at the scene of vending machines. Parallel comparisons set on high alert. Accompanying chances of visual confirmations puzzling the crew members using binoculars. Open waters confused as roads. Content inside of a rumble measured by gauges.

The morning mist extinguished by dust from the now far land of Japan.

Ripple after ripple moving as a rendition of the mast of the ship. Mask painted on the iron to leave a well-accepted upbringing for the eyes of strangers. A slate in disguise found inside. Throughout, an often-used mask as an indication of proportionate off course as a rendition.

Meeting a quota for the markings between the captain and the bosun. The content in the pocket of accepting the deep blue ocean laid unaware during breakfast.

Young changing regrown forecast flew above. Clouds built only for an overcast. Affordable at the generation of the sonar frequencies monitoring them.

An open for sale sky.

An affiliation of a canopy mediated for a long trip inside the luggage area.

Sensory reimbursed terms at the archive of promises from the setup of day two.

Advisory stalemate of liquidated placement around. Bringing up its noticeable duplicity.

An odor of a savior lay overtly since this wasn't carrying any passengers.

Measurable by a linguistic strategy were the fates of *Vessel by brush's* crew members.

Making a proper call is the wait on the steps of judgment of the captain, Huey. Contingency on the plaque for property damage.

An obvious secretary's mole roaming within the radio's frequencies. Influenced by a pattern adding the past's history.

The cargo area reminded one of the packaging of a road's signs.

Chapter 14

377 to 406 Miles

Peering at the left is a locating and benefitting feel filling the edges. Moist from the rainfall that has just recently passed. Steps are etched in the roughly grazed waves for the benefit of visual traffic navigation.

A part of the sea pattern connection is stuck at the keel. Brightness lingers to a squeezed route underwater affiliated with the migration of ocean life. The depth had different beams of blue light seeming to hold a programmed water molecule density.

Chapter 15

406 to 435 Miles

A scuffed mustache meant words. Wanting to be a source of recommendation and seeming careful with his thoughts.

Wanted dollar bills are the rested assured shore.

Favors given for building a more relevant sensation of interior design.

Comparing an iron steel to another the ocean stood again. Thirst mended for the ruin of a quench.

Folding carton marked a resolution of hygiene since the decade of within microseconds it took to complete the arrangement within the cargo area.

Coinciding moments on its trek hushed the bump of hard labor.

'Million curtains opening as a start of a sequence' name found an agenda about paper riddling.

His development; costly at a rolling canister's bearing.

Curves of a permission being asked at the entrance of something pouring.

A pile up of chances on the contingency of cruel men miles away stuck on the crew's mind.

Connected to the postline a filler posted on the heading of a connection.

Thieves by bribery hosted the western pacific drifts.

Propulsion advances an echo that drives matter toward the propellers.

Inanimate compromise falling now and then.

Foxes that guarantee an entry missing.

Puppetry of a theory beyond the numbering patterns used to measure pinpointing allocation from the sitting cruising altitude of the leaser's altitude satellites.

Icons elongated as a set right dominion.

"If the figment of time had something to do with approaching the ground, what would we do once we touch the ground."

Mixes of an adjustment as an ill pact.

Simplicity's exchange on the corners of brushes.

Origins that are dually altered by editions of fame.

Positions of abandonment ruining a post at an outlook at the two o'clock view, nine miles northern heading at two in the evening.

It had been five days.

Paralysis that is influencing the eyesight of what is held.

Heights used to prick the mentality of one squared off a trend of abandonment moments within each crew member's turn at the end of the deck, unturned by the forgery of connection and dismissal of a conclave at the barrier of contingency and a parameter of an opposition. Belts and delightful canvasses swaying in the open wind.

Echoing through the branches was an unseen wind in the tropic making the direction of the ship. A topic of concern at the propulsion of symmetry and adjacent curves. Settlement of a commission as an astute responsibility.

Vicor at the water drowned by the roadside used to enable more stability; an efficient balance concerning a puncture.

Attendance of a composition at the levels at dealings with a cradle of an omission on a foxy term. Parameters of a decision until the outpost was riddled by a maximum prospective make up of council.

Banned and put at an estimation was the crossing paths of three mega ships.

Patterns congruent to a suggestion about sailing heading surfed a pair's schedule.

Ruins embarking under the boat disoriented the sonar navigation system. Postures of a dealing at the outermost que fetched by a term of illicit mark ups.

Combustion of a blamed dent at its shear whistle at the front left side.

A balance for the equipment mechanics.

Bullet points incorporated for a mark within movements of floatation.

Plummeting amazement of a sincere track.

Ports that were left were offering a completion of a fairy tale at the yielding sights of the next attendance.

Solving a riddle that was a mistake in its own entirety, the lights stayed on during the day.

A thirst for the cost of returning to the departing point.

Before concern could engage the perimeter.

Stories like that of an abandoned parish stabilized the courage of the crew mates.

Promises counted from the least ignited reaction of thrill grew.

Inadequate chances to get a full background from each other were openly identified.

Mentioning a structure stories of land and sea began.

One such as the folly at the cliff of chance of an acrobat who did tricks on a cliff.

Admirable parameters of rainfall began, some that could have been similar to covering a golf course.

Migrating muddy thoughts that are uncertain toward finalized attributes was the vowel used down the stepping-stone of the ship's management in a dominant form.

The maintenance of the ship is similar to balancing a globe.

Conversations of a steady time clinch to themselves.

During a hilltop climb unseen underwater, a feel of a windy wave was felt.

Curtained view through split windows shun a gaze into the main decks control center.

The comparisons of an ideal part of an underwater hillside on rough terrain were quickly passed.

Solid grab for participation of hygiene were repeatedly practiced.

Agreed to testify a now hollow and illicit column of values stuck inside the membranes of the crew.

At a course for millennial simplicity, their pride was painted on their uniforms.

Reinforced by a bumping ache, the ego of the captain reflected on the jewelry they were carrying.

Opliet's hoisted a shredding jump at the gates of other oceans.

Suspicious of a thirst originating from a location full of admirable quench.

Populations contrived of a radio frequency call back.

Changing idealistic anonymity through the piercing of daylight.

A mass with a thoroughly inspected past reinspected and moved onboard.

Found in a belt that was holding countermeasures.

Benevolence at a stepping-stone of a peaceful stride.

Connectivity as a pattern of the lighting.

A rough break of times as a median of expenses.

A mission based on a thirteen-listed checklist. Tough break about penetrating items on economical counts

Chapter 16

435 to 464 Miles

Mentioning what is inept became a rounded cause of effective efficiency as a burst of programmed anticipation on the cause of a vanquish.

Every inept section filled with the anguish of being on a welded metal spanning on top its alignment.

Growth and a busy personality was the bearing of chests. A lending effort of a turtleback.

Above under surveillance only a storm could permeate the navigating course. Channeling the watching of traffic with a draft.

Concerning 'Conveyance' adjacent to the windlass's commentary.

Counted by a yard an exclamation by Ovas at the last control lighted warnings for a night's shadow.

Against maximizing the growth of a decibel count of a growl channeled by a timberhead.

A thole's disguise as a rupture of the comparisons of Vessel on brush, Opliet, and *Mike does*. Within the concept of time.

Tiller in the realm of commotion. Bankrupt arctic grounds hearing the burning down of erosion beside pacific shores rolled over waves. Without an ease.

Since the crew is lined up to a lining of growth, one similar to asking around.

Rocks knelt at the clouds.

Healing as a delight of a crossroad.

Scent on a terminology as its quantified.

"Supplementary artifacts are a lastly identified premise." This couldn't be a lesser term of efforts towards the column of chancellors.

"Beneficiaries of a cost."

Simply because it knelt for a just partition.

"Mending a relationship." Mockery at the installments of crowds.

"Upscales at the delight of perfection."

"A greater than generous appliance," supplements included at the height above sea mentions.

Found contemplative. A molding plot stated in a mathematical language.

Outside convergence of a harrowing sorrow besides the wheelhouse.

Nominal federation of a plaque.

Ranship composition of gust on.

An alliance for an etiquette agenda opposition for greatness. Turmoil of composite.

Loom of a dusk. Facts treatment. Building on a chest's coverage. An appliance dissolved. Backing an infiltration send off.

Spar motioning a nest's growth. Aboard was the calamity of a voyage.

Limits abandoning a measure. Grounded by a center of decadence.

Supercargo contraption turned out. Anti-traceable Filipino makeup near Xebec while Sulking a situation.

Generosity incumbent as favors fly out wide in the open; the one willing to lead the dry roads into pits.

Available counterfeit over its own.

Fouls contempt enough to reach into the balancing between sane and insane psychologies.

"Ya'll an economy with that same push of a shrew, at the full expectations vowed at the altars of passing luggage." A tone excluding the mixes it takes to turn.

Chapter 17

464 to 493 Miles

Laughter held the cafeteria in a high-density mood from *Mike does* approach in the northern route hallway.

Spirit handled. An accredited forum unprecedented by an allegory of surpassing spectacles. Inside was a decaying growl of joy.

Gold for the remedial pontificates.

Struck a discussion about dismissing the bartender's attention during a cricket match set on the television lit up the crew's cross-oceanic quiet mood. Over a bearing.

Laughter of rejoice followed the comments of independence dictation around Ovas' mind.

An attempt of destruction as an adjustment of frontier. A conductive momentum as it rose. An oppressive turning of a searching and a turning lane.

"I'm going to pour more by myself!" a heard voice; viscous at the moments echoing at the sudden adjacency. Reliving as an itinerary.

Strake elements that withstand a pheromone silking out of ocean life.

Terrain on the ideal of a constant change in the premonition. A state of withdrawal as a symptom of counseling as delight of commission. Turning in an affiliation chances of opportunity. An end off at the molecule approaching a cynical state. An abundance of efforts, documents eradicated on a luscious groom of a landfilling landslide.

Portrayal at the immune projectile of decisive turns. Fast interchanging motives.

Bee's shallow and rhythmic into a maneuver at a realization.

Minus the missing chancellors of an effort about the blue peter's delight.

Dodger accessing the epidemic onto a cognition.

At a stalemate of a conjoining. Opposite and sturdy.

Forecabin plaque applicable on a credential. Saving a rounded advancement.

Free board minimal conditioning at the races of proportion without an ace.

Clew Channeling at the quest of boosted enhancements. Regarding a satire.

Bowspirit cost of a benefit. Outside a civil autonomy.

Cathead system affiliated to the forensic economy while saving effort.

Off to acquitted neon and thoroughly affective intervals.

Camber policies of a decorum near a scene.

Freeboards following a breaking and regarding a scene.

Genoa rocking an astute forum besides its mass to weight ratio.

Starbolins channeling an issue dragged by a track.

By scupper council, a banquet of the officializing point was in control. Canceling an outmost point of posture at the fanatics of those it had chosen.

A trunnel is being used as a minimal secondary assailance concerning outrage.

The condition of a walty left still and dull moment concerning.

A conditional state except a care of the mirage while canceling the yardarm's use.

An unkempt care of coalition.

A situation of a cure.

An ending a moment confessed at a suggestive construct.

Near a chance made out of a becoming and rash idealistic condolence.

Situations of a drag.

Falling on the drapes that lowers a constructed forum.

A nuisance of the paste of nurture.

Conductive memories at the slate within parts that use a grand mention.

While channeling, a quest irrelevant mended for presence was registered.

Backlash on the ports named from 'f' toward 'j.'

Commenting on rounds elaborate enough and confronted by a slate.

Whenever decorations came around a thought resembling 'dedication of an appearance' and 'making a misuse of a parallel touch' would have been referenced for the distance covered in the logbook.

While locating a lasting insert at certain controversy.

"A conditional opportune sequence."

This is the competition denying a breakthrough as a certain conclusion as a gruesome foxy emblem.

"Denial as a fellowship."

A sulk of petition committed itself to a plaque of a call counseling comments. "Vanquished by a settling migration."

Finalized by a cruel setting.

Caused by the painted masks based around a proprietary.

Next to the center.

Above a light colliding with curiosity at its effective longings.

Pattern of the redeemed. Channels of a coalition. Windows washed by the indoctrination of an ailment.

The mode of a victorious trial confided a serious condition of a plausible act as a healing nuisance at optimal consurgence.

Holding a delicacy of the mended. A healing of a session. An occasion of greater moments.

Ports of a close call at the corners of a sigh. Delicious modes of participation. "We thought a crucial significant amount of a rapture could disorient a liberty standing up."

Mended for the coalitions lended median.

A course at the settlement. A center of a frostbitten side.

Posted by the rhythmic plot serious enough for the adjustment toward a dedicated forum.

Λ frame of a crust. Connections of a vaporized slate. Chances eroded by a silhouette of a symphony surrounded by an admission.

The dealings with a cost of an overbite. Built in a response of a conniving proposal.

"Dedicating a formal condition of a promise at the collision of mixed mentioned templates at a grain of the heights at a grudge mentioning a part of compromised as send off to the content module of delicacy and granted healing and a disastrous completion of a grudge at the entitlement of a containment rolling around a catch."

Curves of a position mixed the characteristics melted on a surface settling into a posture of decorum and faint backlash hymns hung by a rose's strain gasping into the heavens at the corner of darkened ponds and tearing sums. A remedy of the consistency under a delicate making on a counter of a passing and dismissal as an opportune connect at the ailment of a consciousness as a thrust carried by dead weight woven at the sides of echoing influence.

Seeming to be an alias of a compromised pocket left the foundation eerie.

Condoned by the isle praise by another by the quest of its supreme state.

A union between an entrance. A trench in the course of an implied forum.

Channeling of a cornerstone. Wishing a chance of an economical storm.

Desolate imaginations parameters of a sound condolence. Hanging winch like the character for a taff rail that subdues an escalation of denial. An aesthetic promise conceived by an illusion of a sequence radiated.

Coalitions inside. Noises dedicated to the sly efforts.

At a pattern of influence. Afflictions on the borrowing type.

Commending an outright pour. A conditional exchange at the escape of waves.

Evident at the close entirety of count. Channeling communication at the demonstrations.

Desolate monuments left untouched. Miraculous with an affection to an opening.

Broken evaluations with a delirious amount of connect as a set of delayed conformity.

Following their trail left a pattern of an incisive jist. A symmetrical beverage based on an ailment served daily.

Condemned by the jist of conquest. A gratuitous commenting screams. A forceful optimal conquest arrived by chance as an aiding posture of a settlement of a consciousness. A positive redemption gratified by the outlance of a section.

Down given a lasting call by a barricade. Skysail's wind adjustment put into focus.

Jovial at the parts taken off. Barren at the anxiety that follows each meter covered.

Boasting an affection of possibilities. Adrenaline at the commission of possibilities arranged into an effective kinetic upfront arrangement.

Systems of the crumbling connections. A heated monument of a decay and a selling point.

As the term brought by an anguish. Bonus of a convent. Ways of becoming at a craft's doomsday. Dealing with an acronym of a fellowship at the consistency linked as an approach for the conscious into tolls regarding a fathomed way.

A colliding spectacle. An opponent of crucial delights of an appraisal.

Favorable commentary at a satire. As a council of generosity, compliance wrecks of a justice compiling and in attendance. A royal echo of an opinion of thirst started an inspected treading of a flare.

Chapter 18

493 to 522 Miles

Drowning anthem of amphibians corrected the sound of the engine as the sun set.

Staysail marking an element considering a statistic for the necks stooping outwards.

Conventional affection grazing the start of edges above water.

Solemnly acquiring a sensation.

Too victorious as a decorum. Reconstructions sternpost whimbing through and toward its escalation.

Trunnel; a pattern of affection underneath. A furious chemical leaping in the adjustments of a compromise.

Via Believing as a chance while quitting the windlass.

Commenting on a true forum. Channeling a disoriented ascension at the matter of prosperity.

"We'd go covertly," a matter of terms enduring between two.

Connecting a forum of a chance.

Snotty backlash above a sighting of the conglomerate bandits editing an ascension near.

Vivid display. Content above the commission. On the quest used to practise. Nominal concerns roaming around the slack of tremor. A location primitive to the anguish participating through a response.

Vocal as a proportion to delight. A simple turn of admiration. Reading as a sent pattern.

Beacons rounding up. A bundle in the tracks of value. Choices added as a decorum grows.

Selling a chance. Reigns of an outward essence contradicted by a pinpointed slate.

Eskimo collar masks walking around the ship at a stand of biometrics involvement.

A spinnaker touring a sly nook past the blue painted door east of the nose heading of the ship. All tremors of the abandoning collect forum of astute.

Excluding demeaning colors of porridge with a primage.

Following the coordinate of a yawn.

Following the indulgence to the parts of counter pieces. A sinister larboard set for the continuance of a growing turn.

Chapter 19

522 to 551 Miles

The garboard's niche at the compost of a bedside.

A dodger beyond the gratuitous amount against all terrain.

Controlled by allegiance.

The boatswain's continuity of an era found aboard.

An accordance of an outreach closer to the comparative places of action.

Content borrowed by fish.

Elements of an under growth. Send out at convergence at the toast of decorations. Operatives couldn't mark an attendance of a super delight.

Limited selections of what is an escalation.

Jurisdiction as an excrement. An impacted forum as a suggestion.

Subdued by the implementation. Gracious generosity over a course of time.

Fair chance at the consent of a brush. A decision imbedding by the reprisal caught by faith.

A winning streak reimbursed by slots.

Concerned by the matches lit inside of dull clouds.

Secretion withholding its epitome.

Affording a layer of instruction.

Color at the path of rejection.

An agenda.

Opportunity of the decorative.

An acquire of the systematic.

Participations of a cruel moment.

Minorities escaping on the turmoil-ridden carpet.

Makers of a deriving.

Makers upon a structure.

Impending on the aftershock.

Delight on the cause of genuine decor.

Bitt's rough terrain. Expecting a piece of dust.

Ensign of formidable scents. To the corners of a juncture.

Affordable temperatures.

The hawse's tenure microphones were silent. Since the edge of an edition was letting it, an accommodation fused through the air waves.

A keelson's exuberant momentum left a mark. A use of purpose was a convenient way for the pursuit of the kentledge's characteristic.

Holding a mass was the loxodograph's destiny at the oblique unlike any other object.

Moonraker's ridges hoisted roads of the oblique form. Inside a composition of cost were mumbles about offshore commissions.

Painter at the tenure of a promise. Between a miss and a grope.

An understood code was the purser's ruins at the extraction of a policy. Before an entirely quantifiable count was a limit of velocity.

A touching mizzen's reduction saddened by the miss of a conqueror's blame. A cancellation of an emission fondled during still moments.

A Gangway involved in a miss of a remedy made as a count went by.

Upon a great illusion adding a protruding effort.

A mask mended at the sides of deteriorating a dominion sweeping by.

The commission of the fardage left a known image to leap over, alas in the collapse within the brink of time via outcries.

Chapter 20

551 to 580 Miles

Following the captain hooked up comments regarding his experience with sulking moderation camber. A sea cucumber at the incumbescence of an edge at a loin. Controlled by remedies was a decaying scent favoring a hollow port. Points of vectors included in the rhythmic fouls of a concern. Conjoined plasters that dreamed of waves.

At a colored stone is the buntline's commentary values a list of a cushioning halt. "It seems more comfortable after and right before a meal attending the control room except the walk there." Mockery as an agenda of a finest call. Solving a requirement in terms of expenses. Controlled by a dismissal. A contest of a posture at the grounded making of a conventional asset.

Chapter 21

580 to 609 Miles

A brush per advantage. The wind punching the side of Opliet. Pixelated wave at the grids of focal comprehension attached to the bowline.

Saved moments. A confident strum above the water level with an elegant weight carried at a pathway of a sway. Coming to the vests that accompany the frontier sampled a vindicated.

The companionways conditioned yearnings on the petals of the grazed. A composition of a deadeye at its most obscene regard at the condition of moving waters.

Diagram as a painting of the crawling iron. Competition overwhelming a dissociative. As off as ridges at the admiration of conduct. Science at the rouse of it all.

"Jack had a bright cause of a chapter onto imminent wishing of what's counted by granite." Tastie mocked the noises as decorations on the plot of things.

Venues of concept of common insertion. An allegation of a promise and a craft of admissions readily put to a referendum. Seriously compacting a fellowship of control.

Plot of concern eradicated by a jist of amazement.

Sampling a device at the stalk of a moment.

Convulsing an issue derailing on an opposed refraining template.

The lanyards found indicating missions on a balcony with a view into straying into the sea level.

Comparison of adequate derailing a statistic offering with glimpses around the ship.

Primage settling conservation near a jack-cross-tree on an unmarked triumph.

Chapter 22

609 to 638 Miles

With the laveer touch, partners of coast rose. Through vessel by brush's beauty.

The oakum masks of illicit crude connection leapt except for sunrises.

Larboard delight as a gruesome aftermath for Illeck.

A cause at the limits of patrolling.

Conditions above a set program.

Readmission for conquest at Illeck's eyelids.

A moonraker laying parallel at an agenda as a first scene onto the parrel's positioning. A rodeo missing the scent above battery toward itself.

Roach's alleys making up a tradition within an inch.

Forefoot fondled by a trance outside.

Escutcheon sacred parts of concept left admired.

Dyogram's tradition begging for a statute of consistent avoidability into appropriation.

The foremast's wicked moments promoted for a concern but only for the young.

Davit's tension angrily disheveled beneath the flags.

Elements of the burgee hoisting an allegation of conserved compliments.

Bountiful correction for the lectures.

Reviving a mix of opportunity.

Alerts of promise from vessel by brush.

Devices at the edge of compression at the grasp of Illeck.

Utvu, holding a confederation at a lapse.

The cordage couldn't avoid a cost.

Finding the lap consecutive with a demeanor.

"Diving at the systematic off course at an interior on an empty offroad."

Participations on the inlets curled a seeming anguish.

Utvu, looting the grain used for the sentencing.

"Patterns of a commencement of a partly of sentencing a quest."

Misuse of a device's reach as a crane swings.

Plucking a call.

Body's mattering at the jist mixing around the rested plaster.

"Coaxing at the demise of a congruent send off."

Foots lock marking at an illustration of consideration for antimatters grasp on the gripling artifact that concluded a certain forum.

"Hawser!" given straight orders before a denial of a crude seminole.

Outposts as evident on a statute.

Utvu, beaconing a flared in the mentioning of forensic database.

'Capabilities as an undercarriage.'

Lanyard invented for a greater statistic between a sale of theorem and a coalition.

Over and beyond visual confirmation.

Utvu on the western sight.

A one count for believers at trenches.

Forms of a tile. Foils of a denial on the comparisons of a testament.

Basking at the control of minutes.

Chapter 23

638 to 667 Miles

Bountiful temperature measure from the hull section of Opliet.

A most strategic arrangement for the efficiency of navigation laid to waste.

Gracious temptation from Fotrstastie.

Calculated at the incubencent.

Chapters measuring an acre for Rimblae.

Beyond an exceptional gratuity, Fotrstastie laid to waste.

'Consciousness couldn't afford a telemetry of an out of focus digit at the reality of composition,' a favorite whisper.

'Coverage at the scars knit,' delusions of scalps.

'Pestilence at its best.'

Finalized communion on the branch of hanging was Rimblae's fashion statement. 'Concerns at the right look of things,' figuring skyline vouchers on Opliet.

'Destinies of puppetry' a candid slim pouch of a vessel in the tracks of mended for the additional connections of a term, Hemra bold and characterized by a sequence.

Exceptional as a dock of the priceless portions.

Etiquette mannerism.

Masking a proportional liquidity at the offensive stride for Fotrstastie.

A mollusk's one drying panel at Hemra's focal point.

Looking for the important role within Rimblae.

An oblique term is softened generosity. A plaque mended by an overcast assisting in stabilization inside of Opliet.

A formal contrast of an acute angle sounding footstep at its journey while Rimblae assisted in forgoing matters.

Withstanding a petition of a contrast was Hemra compromise.

Mixing a delight of a favorable admission for Fotrstastie.

Chapter 24

667 to 696 Miles

Neon lit ambush was sometimes the summary of *Mike does*.

Commission on platter dealt with Eruq.

"Exploitation of a condemned apparition of a solution of a centerpiece as a cloud by a settling of a connection." A few of them at a concern.

Jovial noises through the hallways mentioned as a cause of pulpit mannerisms.

Just and jocks regarded inside the referendum of sendoff in delicate weather systems that round up an advisory consent.

Mentioning on an apparatus was spoken by Getlet.

Favorable on the concern of an abyss.

Minimal quantifications toward a participation with *Mike does*' crew.

Chapter 25

696 to 725 Miles

Limited circle of belief on Illeck's shoulders.

Minute by minute center forces on Vessel by brush's acquainted in the resemblance as an astute proficiency at the entanglement of occurrence. A limited anguish within the greater kind of admission. Participation of a crowd sourced membership as a rendered mask painted upon a ruin.

Past lenses of a conniving outpost in the dismemberment of a conquest as a tradition.

Complete outpour of a discouraging moisture measured plot again a tectonic.

Controversy as a limited participation. Sudden praise earned from a delightful make ended by interior commentary. Nioler's delicacy and quenching yet most furthermost attraction couldn't have been any more of a decay than its knowledge about him.

Silence froze Mect's undergarments.

An adequate form as a lining opposed Nioler's limit on the jist of a helm.

These stood as parameters of a consciousness.

Chapter 26
An Understanding of Relinquish
725 to 754 Miles

Lost inside dangerous empty sonar readings floated Vessel by brush.

A feng shui epidemic of a proper systematic forerunning statute at a sure thing confronted. Nude selections of information prancing at a palpable conscience. Graft accomplices on the immediately arranged decor as a sensation.

Protecting a critic's scent by a heel of wrecking touch. A bias satire on the conclave that brushes a parameter.

Favorable agendas on its own decorum. Ascension on a controlled effort as a lie in order to participate in the illusion of the night falling.

Sincere upbringing melted at the feet of those roaming a scandalously lost past with stories of those who this ship had traveled with painted within the healing bowels of nuts in walls.

A destined conveyance.

Located by the bases.

Dressed to impress on Vata's itinerary.

Oligarchy of a containment.

Regiment of a slow repeating descent.

Primitive anguish around vessel by brush. A traditional of the opportunities being overwhelmed at the translation of a course needing to be cared at. Positions at the gates of windy boundaries are being used for the chances of quarterly nerve ended reactions. Like a prick molding, a burst resigned for the delicacy recruited for an animal's course of slight efforts.

Contingency of a gist at the breast of confrontation. Marks of an epidemic completed as a swing of proper destiny. Sound of tunes out of the back of a vessel.

An embrace of the slaughter's distant sound via a heroine's strain. Vata, mumbled elements proportionate to a consistency of whale hums. A neon sky waved at everything in reconnaissance patterns. The reach of gravity waited at a compelling position.

Coming out of a reprisal. A freight full of a condoned placement. Swinging to the waves.

Couldn't suspend a taking in of heat.

At the light of day, a piece of metal floated. Rehearsals of evidence.

Commencement approach as an ill ridden fact. Plucks of a generous plaque hung in the name of nautical travel. Opinions as a numbing concession tested by an elaborate chance.

Punctual and dismissive on the crown that rearranges a dull plaster. An ache of arrival masking the crew.

Fastest growing isotope.

Pact in the dusk of proximity envisioned and logged by Vata.

Chapter 27
Denial at the Craze

754 to 783 Miles

It took more to supersize a panicked crew for *Mike does*.

An idle scent of Fau.

Opposing a rationing concern at the grain of opposing lectures. Conditioning foxy touches that leave a bright crest within the warmth of decision-making. A loyal temperate measurement on ice molecules fell above the clouds for the coverage of forecast.

A policy admitting at the conventional cause of doing right. Plates of the count of grain given off as abduction. The making of reality whimpering through minds. Bedar wasn't laying a furnished outlook of things since the victorious want of organization needed labor.

A making of temptation in the open seas as roads continue to run into each other. Repe's counselling about a sequence of traverse mind-bending puzzles was a layer of etiquette added to the floating weight.

Furnished an outermost past. Collections of a commencement of a practical urgency. The brainwaves were being altered by the sway of the ocean. A mediocre of a thrust at the attempt of converging alliances. Alliances prompting a heat on the coverage beyond a dusty sight.

A sighting could control the mechanics of more volatile turns. A layer of nobility painted inside the hue of *Mike does*. A sense that struck its own order as concessional comment at the braces of what lay at contact.

Looting prepared the crew members for watershed responses at pirates. Water turrets and rubber bullet rifles equipped for the aggression of those attempting to infiltrate the ship.

Folly could fall more slower, a perpendicularly absorbing feel from a point of view criticism matched the reality needed to woe a conversation onboard/bedar grew weary at the connections between an absolute pattern against the result and its product that proposes that delight is after the maximized efforts of happiness.

A manned possibility of concern stuck at the ailment producing bubbles on the propeller. Outermost dedications about staying focused characterized by chance. Chances willing to decide the difference between a scene and confrontation.

Marking a connection became a navigational trek. Default symptoms at the calling of lost insurgence at the tongues of crew members. Fau's audible level on *Mike does* was known.

Chapter 28
Collection of an III Specialty
783 to 812 Miles

Binding what was a sled for oceanic fanatics brought to a cruising staircase sequence.

"Out of a jolly oust" *Mike does's* Getlet reminded the crew in front at a visual conscience honestly and holding a sturdy form that was a strengthening force for the long-lost agenda.

Making its way west. Awful insights at the reminders of an inspiration. Locations on the placement of a code. Indecisive mentions elaborate at the tensions of completion.

A form of stamina without withdrawing an incrimination.

Concurrent for Duis who was elated and rational about this.

Affective by the coming from the velocity used to count seaside elevations.

Blessed and branded on the aiding happening by a stood ground. Affiliation from Bedar's background.

Chapter 29
Conditional Manscaping

Kneeling at the contradictions of the sways of Vessel by brush. Making its way east.

Chances found out an alright way to spend personal time with Huey.

"Coverage of an antique." Moments of resting with Utvu.

Pecking in a slate was Huey's way of editing data with Vata.

Commentary on the delight of the concourse resilient and on the conquest as a bouye.

Additional *Vessel by brush's* reinforcements were centered to its location. Nurture of a chill was the roofed weather symptom. Decadence of an item on a propulsion as an admission.

Request of systematic values sent on a decadence's campaign.

Courageous checks of a domain. Grappling on the strange opportunity of a cause.

Effective while Vata was in charge of a brought in item at the gates of dismissal. Greatness of what is acquired on the enhancement of coalition.

Introvert and consciously mended at the partition of a clumsy effort. Values directed to the personality were at ignition.

Assistance for Utvu laid conservatively with decorations aimed at a clue.

Remembering how to leave a conversation overseas. Made up confrontation roaming about the sequencing of a plausible continental. Revision of an outtake as that one brought up.

Opposition in a stain. Sulking of a delay as a decommissioned parameter.

Weeping a conferred way. Woven at limiting the conference. Near the weave are chests upside the crowned mentioning a close contact.

Howling blanks at an edition upon contact. Opposite of an agenda checklist is crawling partially. Extensive moments onto moments put to an end. Over the end claiming an edition of losing focus. With focus that examined visions mitigated on the conference winding into a tale of promotion. Utvu left handling a premonition.

Knocking vessel by brush. A junk of an idle promotion. Sequencing as a mighty gesture of the conceivable act.

Borrowing a scenario. Roads at the participation of a glow. Echoes of a rack. And an endless epitome of a curving gesture, fanning a thrust. Congratulations below the lengthening minute.

Critical pointers. Populous of a migration of the decoration. An affordable minute of an etiquette moment. A majestic extinguished parallelity on an adjustment that crawls by a scenario.

Amusement quenched by Vata in the developments causing static within Utvu.

Chapter 30
Contest at the Engagement
841 to 870 Miles

Boosted parameters as a grain inside of time.

"We are jealous," forms of a delight. Missionary annulment. Decay at the strife of emblems aboard Opliet.

Stalemate aggression. Ill quantifications. A policy of channeling a crust. Mediocre strife backed up by Doe.

Looping consciousness. A pilgrimage landing by a scent. Fault at the layer of conquest. Verifying a sentence for Opliet.

Conglomerate accusations. As a stalemate on the supervision. Reentry of a sly portion. Simple times at the commotion attached to Rumson's voice.

In a waiting moment. Delight at the symptom beyond a rouse decaying with medicine at a precinct. As a proclamation of minors at the range populating a beacon. At the outright satire and sequence of Opliet.

Sorting a chance. Delays on the counter. Breathing dividends. Crust at the frosting. A decadence of a round. Withholding a pattern strange to Doe.

Willing at the centerfold. Forces caught in between a knot strung high above the deck cause an illusion of drift. Monuments of a comparison. To the light of concern making a scene. Mission of the set position. Chances at the collaboration Opliet.

Canister in between the corner. An attribute of the establishment rounded a start of moments. Minuses on the range of premonition as conquest of a properties edge as a cranes swing toward a position.

Limited anguish on the thrust. Loins upon a junk pile. Mended at the attribute in disguise on the hidden point from Rumson's angle.

Below is applicable. Noise being read. Rockets at the essential use of a con. Mockery on the statement as a position of a crown's call. Halting of motions forging a concern within Opliet.

On a concern. Halos drawn by the quarterdeck of the boat. Chances on the columns. Setting depleting. Doe had not accepted a chance of a cause. Mitigation as a crude effort because of my interrogation's affair. Blue leaving make up as credentials fall out. Echo's epitome of encouragement attracting a rash belief of a current.

Chapter 31
Velocity
870 to 894 Miles

Final optimal finessing the evident promiscuous affectionate whistles of *Opliet*. Quest on a rhythm upon tranquil parameters. Rumson's formations of a grouped sensor at an entanglement at the reach of a conniving storage participation delight. Affording a relevance at the camping solution of a participation of a favorable quest with Gollow. Proper admission of the grains that leave marks reaching into the symmetry about a jolting portion away from Eeku.

Connection opposed by the celebratory items of a containment. An adjourned controlling parameter. Finest credential pastures of an overtly near the abaft.

A sensation of decorum of an almighty grab adjacent to bows. Delights served at a nominal curve at a settling mishap. Encouragement at the mention included to vanquish a thrust dedicated toward an optimal quest.

Limiting at the jist of brails with Gos. Optimistic at a correct interruption. Decisive dump as an interaction as a plaque of a recall.

Openly endorsing 'the bulwarks affreightment.'

The chime founded for *Opliet*.

Readied fall on the deadfall bee. Chosen by the idealistic pinnacles with momentum and crudely arranged itineraries.

Rumson's possibility on the fairlead. Connections of a broad syntax released by a term of relinquished proportions.

Bleeding molecules of water on the forefoot bollard.

Wetness around the grapnel.

Jack's compromised bunt.

Moments crossed Gos.

A title that had grooves for a pipeline as the connection of happiness acquired by the buntline for Gos.

An occurrence for populous advocacy of a remedy and suggestive connections.

Abundance as parts of connection for a sea level.

Angelic vision on a sequel of a brand. Absolute result of an abduction.

Minutes of cognitive behavior. Beyond a rise of a marking. Compromised of an insertion. An intellect of proportional descent at the clinch of Eeku.

Positive marks.

Lack of the conquest.

Abundance mentioned by Gos.

Van built by a specimen controlled by an adhesive moment.

A plot for the forbidden.

A cost counted by Gos.

Heels around the dogwatch sighted by Eeku.

A beast on the ocean.

Conniving plots.

Choices succumbed to.

Delight earned in the forecabin.

Competing with a stout genuine call.

Aggression roaming about the oakum.

"Regression of a minus plaque."

Making up port of commentary mentioned by Fotrstastie.

Greater sequence around the frap.

"Required to meet a repoise..."

"...items of a baltic kind..."

"...mentioning a favorable crunch..."

"...best likings of a commenced attribute..." an ascending roach.

Compromise on a contention rate on Hemra's count.

Jolted by a solution by the tranship.

Tampered icon hawse.

An edition for a cause.

A forcefully put opinion.

An aggressive debut.

Rolling above a secondary instalment.

Memories etched the jib.

Turns knocking.

"Everest concerning," illicit commentary by Hemra.

Cons of complete patterns.

Chapter 32
Selections of an Overhearing
928 to 957 Miles

Minute of participation for the lutchet.

Banquet of an appreciation from the keel haul.

Illicit prompt on the iron. Secondary at the occasions adjacent to the lutchet.

Delight on the composition made by the lutchet.

Noise acceptance jack. Favorable take on cases regarding fumes halting the decorating process. Missing a conditional upkeep. A trace at the median of a branch and its outer cylindrical walls.

Loiter being recognized luff.

Annulment of a kilogram. Delicacy of velocity.

Participation in affordability.

Tested by the cozy parts of criticism.

Causing an adjacent blending effect. A packet frozen for the council of communication.

Finest call pulled. Messing up a pattern. Collection of a pivot and decorum. Destined by the insight. Pulleys on a destiny.

Manned effort. Deficit of construction. Redeemed at the point.

Hauling an embrace. Equipped as a subtle convergence. Thrusting intelligence. Leveling an output and opening.

Mentioned by a grasp.

Sulks as an arrangement. "We'd ought to comply with the border written rules."

Openly as a vindicate, "we were a solemnly swearing proportional geometric labeling a pursuant consent. Items on the coalition vindictive to pouches."

While sorting a question rose, "Sulking about a testimony?"

Linking a furnace owning up to the dusting of a vanquish of a paste.

An overly ambitious cause. As a drunk pile up. Collections of a rebellion.

Limiting fragrance. Generous of a plot as a scribe of discrimination.

Participant of a minority of the balancing pivots.

Glorifying decorations of a cause and effect.

Hues from the aurora.

Bundle of affiliations within a balance at a stagnant premonition.

Opening a costly ambiguous slate.

Collective bonnet as an onset and indifference quantifying a strategy used for protocol on an accurate form.

Embrace on a stall and anguish of a vanishing occurrence of a probability beneath an entrance. An occurrence beneath the ocean density.

Desolate agreements for the delight of a make-up with lessons of a minor stake in the measurement.

Chapter 33
Missing You
928 to 986 Miles

Declared missing with a silence squeezed before the rush of panic rose to swim for the attainment of its lifeline. Pointers for a friend every kilometer as a concussion labeled as weight by Illeck.

"Micro subtle mechanics."

Plank that was a woe at the spectacle of seduction. An undergarment of those at an upheaval. A contingency plan for an outreach in an imitation of council. Intermediate absorption on a thermal setting as a variety roaming about the epidemic of a foul. A crossly read plank that converged a statement and varieties tackling abundance.

A question making an outrageous condolence. A savior for the locomotive motion conceived by a tribunal element of prosperity. Deterrence of a mask. Conclusion on an errand put on a sitting pack.

Moments sawn minus signs on the opposing terms contrived of a coalition. The epitome of a requirement being indulged at the scenario of forgery. Comments at the solvent corners broken by bare skin bones.

Dropped thorns dedication of a center of elusive corrosion. Cynical deportation at the sensation of a markup. Characterized on the portions we illicit choice fellowship as a going to the crawling. Characterized by the efforts as a clue is ridden in.

Threading a knight's touch in reality by a dock as an obvious provocation or denial of the crossly knit as a denial of a concept at a thrust of company. Wishing well equipped with a slight mention of participation. Concluded by a remedy. Heights are characterized as indication of great ownership. Chances of the other delight markup and the aisle of confrontation. At the conference of items of a character that is unusual to a brand of chances toward edges and a duration. Threads diving at the route's desks.

Factual questioning, sincerely emotional lit by a well put in an admission. A stature of a division of a practice.

Chapter 34
Valid Occurrence
986 to 1015 Miles

Ovas was missing a term, winsing about a telemetry on the conjoining portion.

Executing a stern posture above the bound. Strands commenting on an acquisition. Channeling an amount of outrageous.

Connectivity on the presentation. Ovas, claims tonight's wept control of a disloyal continuity is for mileage stamina.

Commencing an echoes rendition of a connection. A participation involved with grease and creases pointed at a fanning.

Nicely touched. Connections by the part. An encouragement with efforts of credentials.

Knocking at a placement.

Nearer to night.

Chapter 35
Postures

1015 to 1044 Miles

Illicit ridicule at the motion passed by hues pointed at the bank mesmerized inside plurality Nermis thoughts aboard Vessel by brush.

Nuisance at the fright missed by a slight fret beckoned by guidance. Somewhat nimble as a token of an affiliation; foretold by Nermis.

Mended for illusions.

Nimble!

A representation of *Vessel by brush*.

Nimble!

"That is so great."

At the rampart of a stye.

Docked on, "I'll waste your day."

Limiting poise.

Referendum from actuality.

Dusk within the lights.

Actuality proven at a curve.

Justice mended.

Final accuracy.

Jovial stunt.

Heights woven by Vessel by brush.

Chapter 36
Dealing In by a Friend
1044 to 1073 Miles

Nicely frightening.

Boastly made up. Offended by an aguishing scratch. Bedar and Fau on board *Mike does* admitting into the drench as a plot. Marking every undone strong length.

Curfew before morning. Torment at a treak. Affiliation of a genuine call.

Tasty roast ran up into jaw dropping thirds of a minute.

Minding an effort. Efforts completing a chance of demise. A demise controlled by a delight as a contraption.

Making an illicit act. Commissions of upheaval.

Noisy and built-in thermal seclusion.

Marked up as a treat.

Chapter 37
Posted Note
1073 to 1102 Miles

Pinnacle of demand. A sense of demise of a dusted kind. Perpetual estimate of a grind as a flight's cause by controversy filled flight paths. A sorting of an itinerary through the basis of an afforded flight. Dismissed at an effort on the congruent misuse of partners. An issue has been mishandled out of comparisons. Commission of secondary consequences are the railing bleak long walled affection upon the tremors.

Bouncing heap of a commoner. In the nights positioning of the gesture's measurement on a blink of a concept. Shelves of a traverse and the angular compost on the grind of consequence and chance.

Happily served keel. An inanimate cause of the brochure. An anguish of the reflection of positioning of a collection and the sights of an encouraging branch hanging. Stepping in the conceivable outrageous pack following the creation of the condemnation of a burning flaunt. Items of the viscosity. Pardoning the editions. Banquete trials of manners. Tents under bridges. An encouragement of a pattern of the neighbor's delight. Compost and contingency. A coalition of a round.

Needing a joint treaty. Total input on the contingency mark of a theorem. A turn to the tastes mended of the returns of photosynthesis reflection by the turn of scents bold about a curve connected by the selling of great visual imprints. Minimal possible at the counterpiece and fixing over a discourse of a limber part of connection.

Muddy roaming. Tours of a fidgette and a neon-colored pattern on the grills that fill an opening commission packed in ones to twos to hundreds, and as a term Minimal of a gauntlet mixing at the portions over a device conserving the return of live channeled centerpieces. The lobby embracing at the connection of a proportional suckling of a ghost on the ensemble.

Dumping at tolerance levels. Conjoining of the decoration. A past over the opening of a concrete. A fencing for moments within its construction's heading. Senile mockery over a jump above a cause sent by rush beyond the sensing of abrupt commotion.

Competition on the corners of a bending sulk with a vicious landing on a square patterned texture that was found on its placement of arrangement. Chances through boroughs imagined at the elapsing turn of clicks of a ground of a commenting brush of winds as a part of a commenting adrenaline as a bracket formed a destiny outside the trim a compilation bundled.

Concerns as a dedicated flat counterpiece redeemed on the coding of affiliation. Batteries as contingency on a lineup of the bests. Continuation of a brass sounding ensemble. Vicor prompting a lily found as a solemn activity. Beneficiary as an act of vindictive plate placement.

Forks written on a bubble. Isolation on the compost compounded at the touch of an adjacent pricking swarm of lead.

Mostly positive about the endangering committed while an erosion through bleak counter terrorism affected the boosted outcry pertaining land crossing activity.

Chances cold and new nearing an epitome of drenching reality.

Sorting a balance conforming to an evident pressure of purpose.

Bouncing on a creation of positive match that is equipped by a lateral aimed squeak as a proportion of cause and telemetry of an audience.

Motioning a simple conquest roaming about an aesthetic condition.

Marking a box in front of the forms of an indication.

Passing the opportunity to leave an effort at the trajectory of a combine and sold-out luck opportunities.

Melting what's appropriate over a sequence of an admiration accord.

Chapter 38
Posted Notes
1102 to 1131 Miles

Winding out at the open seas. An insemination thrusting an inbound collapse of affordability. Making a grand gesture at the opportunities populous on a remedy. Illicit comprehension at the conclave at the set of a clouded port. Adjacent measurements as a concrete heart ache. Conventional out post of a settlement of a crude send off. Conditional brushes as a consent moment. Mended upscaling and trusted designers of antiques leaving their labels on a frontier. Elaboration at the stake of countermeasures.

Inanimate voices protruding from the vessels holding a statistic that mentioned a keel. Positioning was acquired at the seams of control. Coalitions of facts bumbled into rhythm of an elaborate commentary. Winds approaching uprightly. These were the open seas.

Chapter 39
The Quiet Center Piece
1131 to 1160 Miles

Locked participation at the illusion of a generous commencement. An active placement inside the rendition of a mediocre orchestra. A lock that is gratuitous enough to leave a bleak minority at reformation. Bundled in numbers as the crossly lit members attend from outside. The maximum plot of chances painted across the scenario. Participation calling for numbers that are eroded by a limit that collects parts of floating compounds.

Located by the transgressed mention. Mentioning a trail on the conquest's shadow. A conqueror at the adjustment of meters completed. A mention that dedicated itself to parts at the overtly missing credential. Trails on the yearning of a complete satire. A regression of a satire that councils an optimal link inside the judgment of yanked trunks. The push and pull that created fashion without judgment.

An option of concern. Contingency at the tremor of a crusty whispering agency. An opportunity of the element as a crease on the appliances. Options put a scale on the mediocrity of adding population in case of an engine misfit. Connected with the alibi options conquering an accompanying valor.

Consecutive make up on the enforcers.

Collection brought up on a stage of commented rights. An astute form mended in within the gates of a rough bridge with a knot adjusted toward the alignment of trust. The texture conceivable to an edition of fondling puppets. The gates had a solemn overtly gush of a rhythmic allusion of casting fear. An environment channeling a milestone of positive composition altered caregivers. Esteemed by a static / hard ground rush to be intertwined with. An interaction that dusted off at the vectors brushing against an opening. Situated at a ground benefitting a commission of formatted practice. Loyal to an esteem.

Coalition of a friction. Nocturnal epitomes of a crude theory rose. Medicinal pointers of a craft at the etiquette of readmission of purpose. Send off at a cognition in an elaborate ascent connected by a layer. Vital engagements as a vivor toward an illicit crunch inside the piece of jewel. Banners attending the mix of production while seduction arrives on a whim. Numbers of a contract in a scent of alignment. A proclamation deserted by the moment of a character. A colossal dimmed as an appointment in a posture directed by winds. Intumescent affiliations at a ruff within matter. Delicate on a rolling and ruining pathway. Productions in the section of a prance. An attendance equipped to maneuver as title of scenery. Systems tactile enough for the admiration of an agenda. A collection that is a battering rink for avoidable hemispheres. Mending a solution that prepares an effort of affordability. Mystery at the cdition used as a mark up for a throttle's emblem. Commenting around for a scholastic void in an instant. Numbering an opinion as delicacy. Rhythmic involvement as a pouch carrying; benevolent attention migrating in the name of a stalemate. A numbered sensation as a promise of a conclave. A rounded start toward outermost sonar readback. Tacticity on the promotion as a device's idea is in networking traffic.

Chances of construction. Mechanics of an approaching set. Readily contesting a conversation. A motion that pulled victorious collections. A characteristic of those affordable. A brink between seconds at the outermost pinnacle of touching encouragement.

Willing to be a semester.

Errors coded for the grasp.

Howling stamina on the construction of kinetic pulls.

Sequenced parts mentioned inadequate platforms. Forcing an edition blasted by competition while congruent at the bench as a study leap for a beam.

Similar aggravation. Content by the congruent. Backing in the resting of concept.

Sent goals. Appehival of a remedy on the contrast. An ambitious contract. A document holding comments filled with concern.

Possibilities of delight. Weigh in on an infrastructure. Chances of a delight too. Settling of a contention.

Chapter 40
Permission
1160 to 1189 Miles

Completing an effort of idealistic counter reaction.

Toils and aftereffects of opposed tacticity on a frame of coalition.

Impending commentary as a wait over the sounds of pitch-black silence.

Compelled to do a trick shot as an indulging set of proclamation settles in.

Confrontation as an illicit dismemberment of contrived acts.

Covered by a sendoff and a grand testament and adjacent clue.

Couches settled in one of the lounge areas swarming around as a chalant adversary. Confided at the assurance of what is plenty.

Chapter 41

1189 to 1218 Miles

Heists made of a conversation's back and forth. An ailing for the frost gathered up of the deck's windows. New systems being built as the voyage progresses.

Chapter 42
Conclave

1218 to 1247 Miles

On a dusty road. Collection at an opening in the disclosure. As a burning flare. In an anguish place at the bottom. Conscious at the continuity of an era.

Given notion. Making up a tradition. A collapse of a cane. Condition of a receptor. Positions of crafts.

Faintly driven artifacts at a ration. An impending clutch.

Mainly affordable.

Roasted brews around a genoa. A glow of a supple time.

Purchasing and acquiring astern. Commenting about a radiant output.

Finest call for the bluepeters as reconnaissance mentioned opening.

Confronting accusation at the burgee.

Bumbling reentry that could sail on about a contradicting settlement. Forced to exchange the ailment of concern.

Sovereign acquired at the grasp of an accommodation. Banded by the radiation of an affiliation growing at the protocol of a recall.

Bestowed crows at the height at elevation. Boosted continuance affecting anything.

Best grossing attribute about a davit. Believing at a statute about the proven and a commentary.

Chapter 43
What is Around
1247 to 1276 Miles

Fiddley away in the rays. An occurrence impending as
a static cause of imminent coalition.

Chapter 44
Plucking an Arousal
1276 to 1305 Miles

Common allegations contrived as a mask on the aiding of a proficient arousal.

Mending an adequate force of coalition and decadence as a guarantee.

Minority report about the gesture of a proclamation of a destiny.

An about term of the gratuitous millimeter.

A rendition of a contemplation of the ground that holds it steady.

Decomposition as a resuming paralysis of a comment condoned by a rash irrelevance.

Partly concluded by a propulsion of great adjustment.

Chapter 45
Edition of Positive
1305 to 1334 Miles

A nickel for every second on a scale finalizing a conversation between a tutor and her student.

"Saddening mines."

"Crafts and sincere troughs," bitts.

"Chutes taken off and congruence at the alliance of reminiscing."

"Camping under drops."

Chapter 46
From Kitchen to Tables
1334 to 1363 Miles

The ship had found its sighting on the coast line. Broken lines in the water.

Appropriate proportions of utter anguish.

Desolate patterns in the weather scanner.

Forks written at a curve under the keel.

Parts of an edition.

Connections of an overall foul.

Withdrawing a portion.

Thrusts engaged on the ending brushes.

Advocating the rhythms of a compelling note.

Astute mechanics as a block from high turbulence.

Changes high up on efforts.

Corners attributed.

An alias of proportion as fact.

Inside the complete candidacy between favorable and needed.

Afraid of a compressing scene filled with the commenting of values considering a latch.

Banging elation nearer and nearer.

Commute at the side of retribution from a fascination.

Commenting at the gasp of extensive surplus.

A brush of sorrow.

Exponential monument at the reaction of bliss.

Formatted battery.

Leased quarrel.

Indexed exits on a champlain's mailing list.

Prone to an exasperating demise.

Pasture headed toward the sun's rays.

Admission of a policy counteracted by a healing moment. Fanning warm winds.

Openly commenting an output of forum topics including 'keelhauling.'

A scene consecrated.

Opposed by an equipment growl for the turn endorsing the use of the jibe.

Serving an inclusion.

Desolate pints of mayhems.

Superb vision on the range.

Concern as an indication on proportion.

Liquidated on the centerpiece.

Backlash contrived of connections at a ballast shambling away from the jackstaff.

Channels vindicated as growth.

Leveling a heap concerned patterns roaming around a senile moment of aggression garboard.

Concerns about a yield.

Position on a circulatory jack-block.

Banished about a vain moment.

Beneficiaries of a collapsing ridge.

Conduct proposed during a lap.

Channeling an outstanding sense of euphoria.

Chapter 47
Another Sunrise
1363 to 1392 Miles

The emptiness of eternity rounded up as a gratuitous leap of faith.

Openly attending an essential motive that backtracks a seceding glow of bubbles in their rush.

Lowly parking a stabilized sharp point.

Forms congruent at the making of an ion.

Posterized peninsulas at a gesture of cause and demise.

Contributing an affectionate paste that has old remedies.

Conveying the idealistic perseverance.

An attitude placed as a demeaning conformity.

Construct at the look caught opening.

A furious gesture on the possibility of confidence.

An alert over the politics and decorations.

A participation's overtly cause on the constitutional carriage.

Avoiding the descriptions.

Overly applying the counterpiece enraged into rash behavior.

A sector issuing deterioration.

Applying an inept cause of tremors.

A condition used for the inference of bouncing sounds. Symptoms of a vector's enigma.

A collision as a posture grew for what withdrew a slate. Channeling at the equipment with a station lent for the bosun at the equipment's recall sequence.

A packet on the positioning of cornerstones.

Beneath an exterior centerpiece.

Hours riding on the growth of sailing an opportune measure.

Linking an insemination. Decoys of an anguish in the elements.

Probability of a collect force. Monuments of a participation.

Sulking toward the buried.

A setting with scenery linking the exasperating taste of ocean air.

In a few condemnations were a duality. Titles as a recount of consent.

An outpour of discouragement. A house of proportionate terms.

A pattern of recorded gestures.

Collections of efforts.

Capabilities of an edition of compromised friends.

Delightful sounds in the distance.

Comparing heights to the flows below.

Contingency as a plaque of the fellow navigation pattern.

Consul inside the main deck. Opportune parameters.

Finding a healing. Covered statements. Continuing a span of injustice.

A seal on the commitment paused as devices. A rock for a little tone originally talked of in the conference room about an overview of things.

Secondarily victorious on its race toward the lonesome destination.

Chapter 48
Those Pointed At
1392 to 1421 Miles

Flagging a height compromised by the lack of sedation.

Standing up for what is cruel and on the border between right and wrong.

An agenda capable of minding its own wits.

An astute form of forbearing.

Executive calls on the trail's traffic.

Connection as a timid foul on the location.

Chances ground and counted as possible.

Beneficiaries collected and examined by life choices.

A pocket full of contempt.

Redeemable outrageous facts.

Conserving the idea of heights.

Yielding at the corners.

Locating openings doomed to fall.

An applicable sense of serenity at the posture dedicated for a gambling use.

Parameters engaged as the statements fell with it's lazaret.

Comparing a jovial time with what happens next.

Considerations at the fine time of decision-making.

Honorable belts encrypted to disavow dishonesty.

Company on the rails that shine a concern.

Pockets within a gauntlet.

Making a heap of what is showing.

Generous applicable content.

Favorable plaques hung by the captain's protocol concerning scenarios.

An item on the desk.

Locating a road.

Looking above the pool.

Kneeling and forcing.

Mistakes and decoration.

Goals and devices driven.

Habits under the call.

Limber condemned fortifications.

Motions of a take.

Sulking into sleep.

Vivid foreign paranoia.

Chancellors owning a title.

Mesmerized by a topic.

Collection of a limit.

Couldn't populate a dent.

Forging a call.

Participations of encouraging etiquette.

Near misses of leeches.

Roads for friends.

Melting outside its own boundaries.

Vectors distributed across the ships.

Plucking a collection around the usage of the sidelights.

Foreign distance enduring with the orlops.

Each member distinguished.

Favorable content. Commenting on the upright genuine feel. Cost of realms.

Chapter 49
Allied Decommission
1421 to 1450 Miles

Barren zero elevation laying as a flat rock.

Since the irons are hard, the antennas produced a unique filter for the reception of radio waves.

Chapter 50
Allure and Alignment
1450 to 1479 Miles

"Fear fetched turn," Bedar said to Fau on *Mike does*.

"Near a pivot," Bedar continued with a pause.

"Bended into a possible fact," Bedar concluded.

Lines perpendicular to the effects of tear glands whispering the voices affording a noise threshold.

Frowning at the limits of accepted turns that turn the docking of conjoining emotions.

Kneeling at the sight of the rays of auroras.

Blinking away from the heat index elevation.

Borrowing the barren quantification sinister to the canes troubling Fau's mental cliffhangers.

Unpin them, Fau thought.

Having the notches entwined at the hard grips of its knots.

Hikes banned by the insufficient counts of walking distances with grasps at its own shadow verified for antique testaments.

Rowdy with the temperate slits formidable and as a pouring grain's fall branching away as lost sights.

"Faus's request is being revered as an order." Bedar acknowledged his own presence.

Remedies poured at the tastes woven to be peeled.

Forcing the determination of boxers and turnarounds.

Felt as an ideal measure.

"Naming and sorting the counts found fraternizing against my most popular wits." Bedar's thouse surfed a wavelength.

A kind regard on a scale of soft-spoken terms.

Humming the notches set to reach a limit of criticism of what it contrived of.

Freezing and maxed out to be bent by its base line.

"Rowdy at the sights built up for tumbling hilltops." Fau fumbled in the control room attempting to start a conversation.

A survey helped by optimizing the request of hues. Dimmed by atmospheric chances of dressing up one's fate.

Up ahead is a table top built by fingertips still clicking in an orchestra with silence as a choir master.

Jumping into the calming foot rubs anticipated by the sulking of one's sulking tongue at the invite of an evening dinner.

"Catapult an effort with a slight push." Bedar's instruction about *Mike does* had a taste of experience covered within the ship.

Justice on the appearance of folding edges.

Echoing at the reflexes handed into the vapor. A final approach. Centered at an instant. Formats upholding the dump thrusting its frost at zero vectors.

Chapter 51

1479 to 1508 Miles

Gathering the effective masses onto the preparation of set.

Gulp at the even setting swimming about at the edge of confronting unmanned questions.

"Passing by a traditional construct of leapt," a thought unknown roaming the decks.

"A miss in the efforts at cornered retrieval," almost being a voice.

Ghostly makeup as a run-on statement decisive aside the limiting fonts of a time out.

"Saving a little for more," almost haunting.

"Curving the desolate mends and readjustment found allocated by the similes of probability and controversial means for the product around its gesture," accepted as a passenger.

Treks of gardening mentioned by their stooping heights.

"Many brightly lit sights," breaking through the demise of characteristic.

A consciousness was minutes away from finding a contrary situation appealing to the opposed terms "Viscosity endurance at where my reach is."

'Verified...' the healing of a sedated participants that had a '...stock amount.'

Valor on the treat conserving a settling mark.

"Gone for the scent of a wait," a waiting aura with literature's studies correspondence with symphonies.

Chapter 52

1508 to 1537 Miles

A fair amount of idealism taken at a fondling around the trysail. Maniac commentary left on land. What lay as a tuck invited by a loyal containment requirement. A determining sequence choosing. Browsing an effort of the remedial publications.

An agenda of a browsing pretense condoning a noise. Cons and affiliations at the break of a spew. A notch remaking the musk of the walty.

Policies of what is coming set in transit. Boundaries confronted by a claim of proposal. Hidden gruff of the topsail inside its mask. Dooming an alignment situated by the isolation offered by roadsides.

Weather's stakes at handing. Conversational accuracy compromised by a statistical tone. Turmoil dressed as calamity outside the connections of visions. A vivacious lock curiosity of a determining session timid with a stern computation. Gold and dynamite of a heist.

Finding a whiplash. Conditioning as a landin. The windlass left by opportunities to displace it. Granted by a nuisance appropriation of a daily fact. Delight defused by a resting amount of entitlement. Noise in triumph to the coalition for a decadence glowing in a symmetry pasted by a juncture at a yield.

Banners still on sale since left abandoned by the management. Devastating unknown sea life. Grown sounds in the frequency of a hum. Millennials feared by a rushing of an indication from a vanishing moment caught.

X rays polluting as a resultant of a vanishing drought. Beyond a proposal. Xebec hadn't found a brush to involve the idea of nurture onboard. Query of a viscous moment.

Chapter 53

1566 to 1595 Miles

Matching the conquest within provocative criteria. Standing effectively as delight. Promotions haven't been disguised and in transit. Whistling with ted talk about monitoring versus processor usage.

Chapter 54

1595 to 1624 Miles

An agenda confronting others. Gesture impending at the foiled efforts and around a stake.

Loiter elements at navigation. Request at the tension of galloping tracks. Purposely found at the request. Coming at the casts of confrontation. A proposal indicated by a travesty.

Limited configuration. Nuisance of a strut.

Tradition from the pier.

Parts falling off a hillside. A round pathway of surveillance. Chances of an emotion to change fate.

Acute stalemate.

Lifts at a pattern.

Bequeathed as an entrance.

Sinister combination. Remodified by a comparison. Understanding that the forks in the sky are painted in by wet paint.

Curved to sooth viewers.

Incorporated and mended for the melting of unconscious scenarios.

Jury's acupuncture at the must of legal standings of this frontier.

Therapeutic by a genius condemnation. Insurrection as a platter.

A set up destination.

Propeller without the thrust given at each water count.

Messed with considering.

Good friends aboard.

Gusts of chaos after via aerial surveillance.

Boveen stenography.

Hibernating as a nomad.

Keeping everything close. Grains counting the imaging of compounds.

Migrating posture. A remedy of noise at the taste that constructed a chance.

Within the visionary and their participations.

Chapter 55

1624 to 1653 Miles

Junk pile vibrating toward a sequence.

At an eye level, the minutes tackling impatience rolled by.

Environmental characteristics painted a figment of contrition.

Possibilities of a concept.

Pointed north.

Affordable chances on a ratio.

Sly wits rowdy about a corner.

Posture about the heap of food used as a settlement.

Turning the insertion of demand.

Bequeathed by the inside of attires.

A plot to divide.

Environment harboring sarcasm into elaborate folly.

Distinguished below radars.

Risky admiration.

A collection of files mentioning the forum of maneuvers.

Held by sacred comfort.

Chapter 56

1653 to 1682 Miles

Immediate readbacks continuing a sonar reading.

Chapter 57

1682 to 1711 Miles

Embroiled as a dedicated crate, an issue delayed by crossly read sequences stood for a stalemate that contrived of an immune doctrine.

Chapter 58

1711 to 1740 Miles

Parts of a construct. An epitome of hallway writings. The recognition of a filament. Construct from a sending off. Parts at an irregular form.

Confessions of an epidemic. At the rise of a markup and unending composition. Readily of an effort of a sat progression. Reactions of the standing bodies acquired by a remedy. A lecture handling a system of an undercurrent subsequent length.

One moment glanced at. Participation in a rolling symmetrical audition. Equations protruding the missing item of twisters.

Adrenaline as a gust. Taste of an accelerated time. Adrenaline woven for the efforts of a time kept suggestion. Denials of a time inside of turmoil.

What lays adjacent is a defining opportunity. A nimble cancellation of a proposal cause. Control and efforts and a testing sequence left suggestive. A frequency as the recipe floats around every locked six cubic feet.

Chapter 59

An attendance inside the remedy. On a body, it is secluded and admitted. It's an effort impacting a needed item listed on a survey.

Toiling away toward an evident gesture. Limited assurance of a possibility. Decadence as a limit of a programing. A distance falling away within a variable term. An assurance discovered as a dedication of posture.

Camping into the harvest. Contingency of an opportune fall. Ferry's loud call across by the pattern of a count. A progression was being led by the rising jist of a hundred stalemates.

Consecrated as an impoverished count of downstream rivers. Vanquishing festivity of an errand disengaged. An opinion as a stalemate.

Ambition coinciding with voice-overs at the static of ambiguous dates. Terms of an historic time. Coincidence from a brought up term. A unit compressing the gratuitous efforts of love.

Remorse on a bent slope gliding for its followers. Supplements by a condition of a loose collection.

Anguish at a static's count. Victorious about an emblem. Reduced format of an engine concurred. Items of longevity's decorum.

Memorable times. A positive outlook of a crust offered. A test at the provision of diplomacy. Whispering on at the reentry of a possible right drawn. As the drenching force is lowered down.

Chapter 60

1769 to 1798 Miles

Other sides came into recollection as a visual cause.

Chapter 61

1798 to 1856 Miles

Ill and craving a tone. A posture involved with a monument.

Chapter 62

1827 to 1856 Miles

Committed to purpose. A decadence of a comment. An advent of proportional acts. Fitting in to pretend and as a decalogue of a lounging assets within a chance as a crowl in the width of the Pacific Ocean.

A compilation of thoughts. A list of thieves.

Impending arrangement. A consequence of a partition.

Needing a sense of response. A responsibility of a courageous metallic compromise. An adjacent device.

Chapter 63

1856 to 1885 Miles

Conditioning on the overwhelming fact.

Past contributing motion.

Make up at the concerned possibilities.

Commissions as an anchor of the controversy.

An ill amount of the posture attributed to malevolent building. Toward the thrust of the heading was a swarm of dolphins. A calling of a greater kind.

Amplified sensations of the turns. Mentions of rhythmic scents.

A chance from the development. Decay of a timid.

Connections of a far cost.

Ringing a setting of mirage photos closer to eye sight criticism.

Chapter 64

1885 to 1914 Miles

United to a market that roams for the free. A fraction of a settling portion of a demise. A relationship into the stepping-stones of accreditation needs.

A scenery of the optimal conquership motion of whip of the outstanding coalition.

Gestures of a road couldn't whisper a draft in the mediocre set effort.

Opliet's control room stayed a figment of determination. Rumson and Eeku opposed the fairway of loud noises.

Considerate values of a regrouping etiquette of an enormous.

Nearing a title of a section.

Relinquished as parameters, efforts are the urgency of things. A device of a promotional output.

Chapter 65

1914 to 1943 Miles

Curving agendas as an opportunity to revolve as a distant motion. The definition of now on the characteristic of an upscale pivot. Property on the counts that inspect a loud admission.

Chapter 66

1943 to 1972 Miles

Proposed cruises on the indication limited to a valley side tree line.

Chapter 67

1972 to 2001 Miles

A delicate pattern of indulging the makeup of a conscious construct.

Chapter 68

2001 to 2030 Miles

A denying reputation lost at the control involved by an admission.

Chapter 69

2030 to 2059 Miles

A nurture of prejudice at the genetic makeup filtered at the invisible roads.

Chapter 70

2059 to 2088 Miles

A mission at the travesty affairs involved a practice of imploding talkers.

Chapter 71

2087 to 2117 Miles

A match made with no effort. Confrontations mixed in with an olive color melting at the course of a decade.

Chapter 72

2117 to 2146 Miles

Malevolent conditioning above window seals.

Chapter 73

2146 to 2175 Miles

Fanning away as a crossly knit mayhem.

An ever-rested base of symptoms.

Condoning the transgression pointing out a fast built building.

Built sturdy by the contemplation of the crews.

A thorn for the condemnation.

A plaster for devastation.

Chapter 74

2175 to 2204 Miles

Congruent moments accepted as feasible acts. Mended apostrophe.

An agenda for council. Valuable allegiance at a thrust.

Chapter 75

2204 to 2233 Miles

Opliet's roll was an angle of a triad. As a belonging, it leapt toward unusual remedies of the map. It had strayed away from its path. Navigation failure compromised its arrival time.

Conglomerates at the angle of an etched fence. Equipped by an ailing tremor of contingency. Withdrawn symptom above a settlement. Compelling counter insurgence.

Compiling efforts at the rounded accuracy of adjacent mannerisms. Leveled stern warnings inside the distance.

An accomplice for the angular rate of count. Asymmetry of an instruction. Value in a road. Bumbling brinks of congested vocals. Failing a systematic preparation.

Chapter 76

2233 to 2262 Miles

As a fire settles down, so did the goals painted in by the decorations angled toward the safest end of things.

An ailment by the furious contest of standing up is a vowel that reaches back at the decks with wind shears measuring an incapacitating term.

Chapter 77

2262 to 2291 Miles

Strut elements of a rectifying abundance.

Chapter 78

2291 to 2320 Miles

Branded by a suggestive contribution at the nailing of locations.

Chapter 79

No Mileage Covered

Patterns involving an ascent of velocity marking an etching.

Chapter 80

2320 to 2349 Miles

Shredded by the mastery of arts.

Chapter 81

2349 to 2378 Miles

Numbered coordinates evaluating a time toward a spill. Within restitution, the ocean held the fleet.

The altered thoughts funded by the touch of the boatswain congested into chronological orders of three or two.

Engagement in the tracks of a demented term.

Endless abrasions on the ships. Overflying ports messages missing the antennas. Adjacent crews with intellect about spare parts.

Destiny in the glorious points of demand. A second drift inside one of many. Aside the abaft was a clean area conjoined to the others at square feet.

Milestones encouraging an element set at convoys. Managing an included test over a ladder in its own centerfold. Noise of a coincidence.

Chapter 82

2378 to 2407 Miles

Comments about a rational sequence introduced by a light. Clues left as a random port. Channeled parts of a congruent dent.

Beacons for earth. Connections from a rough end. Mediocre chances to an anchor. Moments that were an upheaval to stamina.

Sounds of jokes traveling through the air. Boulders drenched underwater. A feign at cause and effect.

Chapter 83

2407 to 2407 Miles

Puppetry at the highest level.

Illusion's breakin' vows.

Confident match making linguistic pandemics. Official cause and effect affecting a milestone. Contents and a remedial foil of time. An additive of thrust.

Overly delaying the consecutive domino effect of time. Dark hymns from a sound place.

Brails of the needle clan forced away from civilization.

Chapter 84

2436 to 2465 Miles

Capes passed by from a distance. A freight of iron ship whimed through day and night. Hallucinations put at bay by the silence of the ocean. Ocean life flying through the boltrope.

Rolling into a space. Beating to the hum of waves. Bright at night. Stolen at sight by the light of day. Following the scent of the arrival.

Noisy stars. Conjoining a link of a tale. A mechanism by the breams. Read by the navigators.

Chapter 85

2456 to 2494 Miles

A signature of a sighted path. Motions of a connection.
Daily maintenance. Upscale security.

The bulwark's strain fondled as flexible.

A bunt at a scenery's acclimation.

Chapter 86

2494 to 2523 Miles

Cables used to clinch the sides of gliding sides.

The sight of the camber left an enhanced protocol around.

Chapter 87

2523 to 2552 Miles

The bent cable's sighting stood out as an item used for decorations.

Viscous readback from the boss spirit.

Making up positions for breams.

A suggestive bow included in the pattern.

Chapter 88

2552 to 2581 Miles

Silencing the bilge with night stories.

Rigid plaques.

The navigation system of *Opliet* had failed. A hundred and twenty-three miles from set destination.

Banning a symptom near the abaft.

Matter in the shadows of inanimate hulls.

Chapter 89

2581 to 2610 Miles

Possibilities bearing and ranging at a statement declaring that "Getlet is an enormously grinding cocoon."

"Limited sadness by a mediocrity of an affiliation," the winds drew. Steady rhythms of a nocturnal astute forum concerned by a televised connection accompanying a readily posture of conservative.

"Pastures included in the stabilization," they continued.

Concluding to the listener that "making a cross between an inline indentation rather than a culpable."

As the crossly bred sleighs downed a price varnished at the stale count that is leaving a fine line.

Fighting with a roar in order to leave a reflection amidship.

A beacon hitting of the bitts. An angle for a recipe.

Controlled substance at the direction paired with the lines of navigation.

Chapter 90

2610 to 2639 Miles

Halos of clouds marking the way.

Chapter 91

2639 to 2668 Miles

Vessel by brush's impact on ocean life was a sequence. Conversational assumptions as an overall suggestion. Numbers inclined to locate the pathway. Members onboard senile to illusions. Nermis held wits of foretelling to the thud of sea level.

Delight for the protocol of a boatswain. A borrowed term of a scent mesmerized a latch of positioning. Propeller chatter underwater. Mect assumed the call of time was a following of research.

Surroundings becoming a nonchalant hue. The stars as a rush. Founding another chance. Nioler stooped over benefactors and growled over criticism.

Chapter 92

2668 to 2697 Miles

Going into a mode that leave attempted evidence.

Echoes differentiating a calculated poise.

Vessel by brush marked its arrival.

Kneeling in for a gesture woven to knit between the threads that were blown away for an effort to grind out awful matters.

Embrace as a statistic of collision.

Decor filling the scent.

Built on an embrace.

A fanning over a trace with efforts.

Mended to be obsolete.

Leveled as a restriction of compliance.

A match declining its fume.

Chapter 93

2697 to 2726 Miles

Turning as a plaque of condition.

Applied symptoms of a struggle.

Jurisdiction in the fences of conservative alignments.

Cabotage's perimeters entangled by a scent of sight.

Amplified at the contract roving about the emblems decoding a referencing triad.

Kit bow light and put on a sensitive floor.

The roaster rocking back and forth.

Condoning what is placed on an element.

Participating a commission of a portion.

Admitting a stalemate of a cushion.

Applying an echo for the tale that hurdles these crew members.

Efforts of a crossly knit part.

Chapter 94

2726 to 2755 Miles

Elevated point of views.

Irrelevant patterns disposed.

Heels on the top.

Sudden motions pointing at the clew's roast.

Character at the poise affiliated in composition.

Postures reimbursed.

Vivid scope adjusted to the selling of an importance.

Foreign scent of the demurrage.

Fever not raised as a makeup.

Alliance as a trolley rolling on a destiny.

Constituency on a mark of a comforter.

Postures diluted at the order of reliance.

Liquid spanning the left horizon.

Appliance as a complimentary statement.

Collisions avoided.

Giving off an agenda in order to start the ticking of time.

Jitty reflexes as a turn of effort.

Contempt rights at the delicacy of outright demotion.

Revered consumption at the take of a council.

Tracks of surplus whispering while leaving an oozing touch behind.

A crest overpowering the panning bow's allied effort.

Moments found at the cathead's strum regarding a limited boost.

Idealism brought back from the past by the dogwatch's hue at a still mark up.

Chapter 95

2755 to 2784 Miles

Whispers and loud accents inside the wind harbored by the flagstaff's indulgence encompassed by a treatment dually arranged before conscious cons.

Chapter 96

2784 to 2813 Miles

A bunt kept neat for the surety of sea communications.

Chapter 97

2813 to 2842 Miles

Observers leaping to an older formula of finding.

Chapter 98

2842 to 2871 Miles

Compromised by an amount headed at the creation.

Chapter 99

2871 to 2900 Miles

A formidable amount in order to rest.

Chapter 100

2900 to 2929 Miles

Mike does was second to arrive. Equipped with a luggage of a forum.

Chapter 101

2929 to 2958 Miles

Tones of a remedy ballaster. Cause and effect of bits.

Deflection shapes similar to that of a bosun's tangled rack.

Relinquished fuses of a stunsail. At the horizon were the hills of Alaska.

Trench the watching. After angles of maneuvering the chances of arrival heightened.

Readily knelt royalty. As they got closer, they could see anchored ships; *Mike does* and vessel by brush.

Impending pinnacles of affiliation inscribed by the genoa.

A synchronous moment for a hawser.

Opportune memorabilia at a liking of a jackstaff.

CPSIA information can be obtained
at www.ICGtesting.com
Printed in the USA
LVHW041211180423
744575LV00010B/495